Run Baby Run

D. Sabia

This is a work of fiction. Names, characters, places, and incidents either are the product of the author's imagination or are used fictitiously. Any resemblance to actual persons, living or dead, events, or locales is entirely coincidental.

teneyckdani1@gmail.com.

9798860685994- Paperback

ANGEL, *AHEM* FRENCH KISS

AND TO ALL YOU OTHER DIRTY, DARK MINDED BITCHES, HERE'S ANOTHER FOR THE SPANK BANK.

TABLE OF CONTENTS

COPYRIGHT © 2023 BY DANI SABIA 2
TABLE OF CONTENTS 5
CONTENT WARNINGS 7
RUN BABY RUN 8
PROLOGUE 10
CHAPTER ONE 12
CHAPTER TWO 17
CHAPTER THREE 20
CHAPTER FOUR 24
CHAPTER FIVE 28
CHAPTER SIX 31
CHAPTER SEVEN 35
CHAPTER EIGHT 40
CHAPTER NINE 43
CHAPTER TEN 47
CHAPTER ELEVEN 50
CHAPTER TWELVE 54
CHAPTER THIRTEEN 60
EPILOGUE 65

COMING SOON 66
ACKNOWLEDGEMENTS 67
BOOKS BY THIS AUTHOR 68

CONTENT WARNINGS

All of them. Seriously. But here's a few.

Non Con

Dub Con

Forced Piercings

Knife Play

Stalking

Kidnapping

Hunting

Blood Play

And sooo much more...

RUN BABY RUN

ALEC

I ask for your forgiveness, father, as I am about to sin.

She's my addiction. My drug of choice. Mine.

But she doesn't know that. Yet...

But come Halloween night, she will be mine.

Even if I need to hunt her down, Hayden Macey will be mine.

Run baby run.

HAYDEN

Everywhere I turn, I feel like someone's there, watching me.

Watching every move I make.

And just to make things worse, I have to work the night of Halloween at our town's haunted carnival.

No matter where I run, where I hide, the feeling is always there.

But now I'm not so sure it's a feeling anymore...

PROLOGUE
HAYDEN

I stumble out of the house of mirrors, panting heavy and shaking. I look around and Adam is nowhere in sight. The fuck Adam!? I look for somewhere to hide when I hear footsteps behind me quickly approaching.

"Fuck," I whisper to myself, taking a deep breath. I scan my surroundings. And my eyes land on the corn maze. I dart towards it. Hoping maybe I can lose him in there. Once I make it to the edge, I push the stalks down, trampling over them as I try to enter it quickly.

As I get further into the maze, I stop and listen. When I don't hear anything, my body relaxes a little and I take a deep breath. But that was short-lived when I heard laughing from the edge of the maze.

"You can't escape me, baby," the deep voice echoes through the stalks. I hold my breath and slowly look around me, trying not to make the stalks move or crunch.

Footsteps echo around me and I can't pinpoint where they're coming from. How the fuck is he doing this? I spin around in place, looking for any movement.

The footsteps stop and everything goes silent except my panicked pants.

"Run Baby, run," I hear right next to my ear. He's right behind me, his warm breath tickling the side of my neck. Without thinking twice, I do what he says. I run.

CHAPTER ONE

HAYDEN

Everywhere. No matter where I go, I feel someone's there. Watching me. Waiting.

But why? I try to think of anyone I could've upset somehow. But I'm drawing a blank. Maybe I'm overreacting. Yeah, that's it. I'm over-.

"Hayden, are you listening?" Kenna says, pulling me from my thoughts. The clattering of plates and silverware and voices of the crowded lunchroom fill my ears. I give her a little smile and she sighs, shaking her head.

"I'm sorry," I grimace across the table from her. Still shaking her head, she stabs her salad.

"What are your weird senses tingling or some shit again?" She asks, rolling her eyes.

I sigh. "I'm not Spiderman. I don't have spidey senses,"

"Well, you're acting like you do. Dude, you've been acting weird ever since you came back from that insane church camp your aunt forced you to go to.

She's not wrong. That's where it all started... The feeling...

"I don't know what to say... it was a weird experience," I say, shrugging my shoulders. My aunt is a big part of our little town's church, and when she heard about the church having some bullshit camp, she decided it'd be good for me to go. She was wrong. All it made me do was question and hate myself more.

"Anyway, I said that we're volunteering at this year's Halloween Carnival," Kenna repeats what I didn't hear when I was in my head.

"We're?" I say with a raised eyebrow.

"Yes, as in we. As in you and me,"

"I know what *we're* means Ken. But why do I have to?"

"Because it'll count towards our senior community service,"

Ugh, fuck. That's right. You'd think being a senior would be quick sailing. But nope, ya gotta do all this extra bullshit to make everyone happy.

"Ugh, fine. Whatever," I say, taking a deep breath.

"Good. Anyway, back to the church camp convo," Kenna says with a grin.

"Ken, I don't really wanna- "

"Was he there?" She asks.

I look at her, confused. "Was who there?"

"The preacher's son, Alec,"

Oh him. The preacher's son, who is so beautiful it should be a sin. His skin is the perfect shade of tan. His hair? Dark brown, almost black, long on top and short on the sides. His eyes were a beautiful blue that'll hypnotize you. Jaw line that could slice and dice anything. Now I sound like a stalker. Fuck.

In addition, my camp counselor was none other than the preacher's son she spoke of, and I had no choice but to talk to him every day.

"Oh him, yeah, he was there. He was one of the camp's counselors."

"What?!" Kenna says, slapping her hand on the table, creating a loud clapping noise. I cringe and look around at students whose attention she attracted.

"Ignore them. Tell me, did you talk to him? What did he say? Is he single? Dating? Married?" Kenna rapidly fires questions at me.

"Jesus slow down. We didn't really talk. I only saw him a few times, and we only exchanged hellos and how are you's," I lie.

Kenna looks at me with an unimpressed facial expression. "Really? That's it?"

"Yes,"

"The fuck Haydennn," she groans.

"What?"

“You didn’t learn anything about him?” She whines.

I roll my eyes. I go to speak, but the bell rings, saving me. I stand and toss my garbage, then sling my bag over my shoulder.

“I’ll text you,” I say to her, spinning on my heels and heading towards my next class.

“Yeah, yeah, whatever,” she says, winking at me. “Oh! We gotta meet Mrs. Reynolds after school to go over the plans for the carnival.”

“Greattt” I draw out. This is fucking great. Now I have to walk back home because my aunt is attending a party at one of her church friends’ place. I pulled out my phone and squinted at the screen as I checked the weather for later on. Once it loads, I see the little storm cloud icon. Shit.

CHAPTER TWO
HAYDEN

"Are you sure you don't want a ride home?" Kenna asks as we walk up to the school's front doors. I nod.

"I'm sure. It's 20 minutes the other way for you." I reassure Kenna and myself.

"Okay" She nods. We get to the front doors and walk out. The air is heavy and damp, but it hasn't rained yet.

I look over at Kenna and smile. "Maybe if I'm quick enough, I'll beat the rain,"

"Good luck with that," she snickers. "See ya" she says waving

"Buh-bye," I say and wave back. I turn towards the direction of my house and start walking. I live twenty minutes away, well if you're driving. If you're unlucky like me and walking, then I have no idea how long it takes. Can forever be the answer?

Because the way my knees are feeling right now, it's been forever.

I don't know how long I've been walking for when a raindrop hits my face, snapping me out of autopilot. I stop dead in my tracks and look up. More drops hit my face at a quicker pace. Then I look around and notice that it's dark, darker than it was when I left school.

"Fuck me," I mumble and pull my phone out, switching on my flashlight. I jog slowly, hoping the rain will pass quickly.

Once I get a few feet down the road, the temperature feels like it dropped by ten degrees and the hairs on the back of my neck stand up. I pick up the pace and glance around. I see nothing but the forest wall that outlines both sides of the road.

The feeling crawls up my spine, sending uncontrollable shivers through me.

"Fuck," I huff and come to an unwanted stop. I struggle to breathe and look around again, trying to always be aware of my surroundings. I scan the woods and my body freezes when I catch a glimpse of what looked like an orange light behind a tree.

"Hello?" I say like an idiot and cringing at myself afterwards.

"Hayden!" I heard someone say, followed by a horn.

My focus on the light caused me to miss the car that was slowly pulling up next to me.

"Hayden! Is that you?" someone asks. I take a step back and look inside the car.

"Adam?" I say, kind of recognizing his face that's lit by the dashboard.

"Yeah, do you need a ride?" He yells out the window. I scan the tree line one more time and see nothing. I sigh in relief and look back at Adam.

"Yeah, a ride would be great."

CHAPTER THREE

ALEC

I tilt my head a little to see past the tree I'm currently crouched behind. After seeing the glow of my mask, Hayden looks around, fear and panic glowing in her eyes. The rain comes down harder, only making her situation worse.

She walks faster and tries covering her face from getting pelted by rain. Turning off my mask, I attempt to get behind her, but I see headlights approaching.

"Fuck," I mumble before jumping back into the woods. I crouch behind a tree and watch as the car slows down next to Hayden. It stops, and she walks up to the window. I dart behind another tree, getting closer to see if I can hear their conversation.

I can barely hear a thing because of the heavy rain coming down on us.

"Adam?" I hear Hayden say. Adam? Who the fuck is Adam? I sit and ponder for a moment. Shit, it's probably Adam Clayton. His mother and father come to my father's service every Sunday. The service in which I've never seen Hayden attended, only her aunt.

In fact, I've never seen Adam and Hayden interact. Well, I haven't seen them interact in the five almost six months I've been watching Hayden. I've been keeping an eye on her ever since I laid my eyes on her at our church's summer camp. The moment our eyes met; I knew. She was the- WAIT A MINUTE, WHY IS SHE GETTING IN HIS CAR.

"Oh, you're being a very bad girl," I say with a smirk as I watch them pull away.

I pop out of my hiding spot and run to where I hid my car. I jump in and start it up. The tires screeched as I pressed the pedal to the floor and accelerated onto the rain-soaked pavement. I slide a little when my tires hit the pavement.

"Shit, shit, shit" I shout as I correct the steering wheel. I get my car under control and speed down the road, catching up to them. I follow them, but not too close.

I follow them until they turn onto the street Hayden lives on. I keep driving until I find somewhere close to park.

Not finding anywhere, I say fuck it and park on the street in front of a random house. I have a clear view of Hayden's front door from this angle. I watch as she gets out of Adam's car. She says something and waves, then walks to her front door and slips in. That's my good girl.

Adam lingers for a few seconds before pulling away. My gaze shifts back to Hayden's house as he disappears down the road. As the lights turned on, I catch a glimpse of her curvy figure passing by the windows.

I jump in my seat when there's a sudden knock on my passenger window.

"Alec? Is that you?" I heard someone say. I lean down to get a better look at who it is.

"Ah, Mary-Ann. How are you?" I say, rolling down my window after recognizing her.

"I'm well, thank you, but I noticed you've been parked here for quite some time. Is everything alright?" she asked with concern.

Thinking quickly, I grab my phone and hold it up. "Oh, everything is fine. Just pulled over to send a few texts to my father. Not big on texting and driving,"

"Oh, alright." She smiles. "Oh, will we be seeing you at the carnival Friday?"

Oh, I'll be there. "Yes, you will," I smile.

"I'll see you then. Have a good night, dear. God bless," she smiles.

"God bless," I grit through my teeth. She turns and heads back to her house. A sigh of relief escaped from my lips. I put my car in drive and pulled away from the curb and head towards home, thinking about the things I have in store for Hayden.

CHAPTER FOUR

HAYDEN

"Do you need a ride tonight?" Kenna yells from inside her closet.

"No. Adam said he would give me a ride home," I answer from where I'm sitting on her bed. She pops her head out of the closet, grinning.

"Adam as in Adam Clayton?" She grins.

"Oh, shut up. It's just a friendly gesture," I say, throwing a pillow at her. She dodges it by jumping back into the closet.

"Sureee. Any-who, wear this," Kenna says, holding up an all-leather outfit she pulled from her closet.

"I'll just wear this," I say, pointing at my outfit - black leggings, combat boots, and a spooky sweater. It's festive and cozy. Right?

"Girl, no. It's Halloween. We're volunteering at a Halloween carnival. Come on now," she pushes again.

"Ken, it's fine. And we're not even the same size. If you haven't noticed, I'm a lot bigger than you," I counter.

"Oh shush. You're thick and beautiful and sexy. Which is why my next pick is even better," she says with an evil grin. She disappears back into her closet and comes back out with the outfit and my jaw drops.

"No fucking way. Nope," I say, putting my hands up and shaking my head. "Kenna. How and why do you have that?" I asked, shocked. She shrugs her shoulders and flips it around, looking at it.

"I made it and because I wanted to piss off Bailey's parents for basically calling me a slut,"

"You dressed up as..." I pause for a moment, staring at the outfit. "A sexy nun?"

She laughs. “Damn right I did! Walked right in that church Sunday morning with my head held high,” she says, recreating her walk. “I wish you were there to see it. Not that shit camp.”

“You and me both,” I sigh. “But seriously. Not happening,” I say, pointing to the costume. She grins.

“Oh. It’s happening.”

“Kenna, my aunt will KILL me. There’s no way she’ll let me live after seeing me in that.”

Kenna sighs and throws the outfit on the bed and plops down next to it. “Hayden, when are you going to realize that you’re not here to make the people around you happy? Are you happy? When was the last time you did something for yourself?”

I freeze.

She sighs and shakes her head. She looks down at the costume, then back at me. “Can you just try it on? Then I’ll stop annoying you.”

“Fine,” I say, quickly reaching for it.

"Yes!" she shouts, fist bumping the air.

I turn around and undress, then I grab the costume and start layering it on. Kenna comes over and helps me adjust it. Once it's on, I turn and face her. Her jaw drops and her eyes grow wide. I turn and look in the mirror on the wall.

"Yup, you're wearing it. Sit down so we can get you ready," she says, pointing at her vanity chair. I don't argue and do as she says. Because I deserve a night where I don't have to hold back and just be me.

CHAPTER FIVE

ALEC

Being the preacher's son comes with its pros and cons.

Pro: People respect you and would never suspect you of any wrongdoing because you were raised as a good little church boy.

Con: Everyone and their great great grandparents know who you are.

I parked my car in a shadowy corner, keeping a close eye on the entrance to the carnival part of the festival, eagerly anticipating her arrival.

Finally, after almost twenty minutes, she arrives. My cock twitches as soon as I lay eyes on her. Her and her friend are walking into the entrance. She's dressed as a nun... a sexy nun, to be exact.

The veil and cap gently rested on her head, covering her hair. The neckerchief is covering her beautiful neck, and fuck. The skirt of her habit stops just above the knees, and she's wearing black stockings. With the combination, only a sliver of her thigh is showing.

The more I stare, the more my cock grows harder. I adjust myself and grab a few things before stepping out of my car. I look around before making my way towards the carnival entrance.

I hang back, keeping some distance between Hayden and I.

"Alec! It's good to see you here, son. How are you? And will Father be joining us this evening?" I hear someone ask from behind me. I put on a fake smile and spin on my heels.

"Ah, Alvin. I'm well, and no, he will not be joining this evening," I say.

"Oh, no? That's a shame. Well, let him know we will see him Sunday at church," Alvin says, putting his hand out for me to shake it.

"Will do," I say as I shake his hand. We part ways and I get back onto Hayden's trail.

I watch as she weaves in and out of the crowd of people heading towards the house of mirrors.

"You sure Adam is bringing you home tonight?" her friend asks.

"I'm sure. I'll text you when he picks me up, so you don't freak out," Hayden answers before they split ways.

Adam's picking her up, huh? I'll have to change that.

"Tonight's the night baby," I say to myself with a grin, and then I find the perfect place to sit and wait until the carnival is over.

CHAPTER SIX

ALEC

I watch as Adam pulls up and parks his car near the carnival's entrance. I chuckled. Show time.

"Nah dude, I'm just tryin' to pop that cherry of hers. Fuck dating her. I'd have to spend too much money on snacks and fast food," I hear Adam say as I make my way to his car. I feel my anger rising.

"Bro, she ain't *that* big," I hear someone say through his car speakers. He's on the phone. Well, this is about to get a lot more interesting. I check the time on my watch. The carnival ends in exactly twenty-seven minutes. I can make that work.

"She's kinda big, bro. But she's got a nice face and a sexy pair of tits, so," Adam says, laughing.

Clenching my jaw, I pull down my mask and switch the light on. Then I grab my switch blade from my coat pocket.

Adam is still laughing as I approach his rolled-down window. I knock on the side of the car, grabbing his attention.

Jumping in the seat, he screams, "What the fuck!?"

"What? Adam, you good?" the person on the phone asks.

"The fuck is wrong with you man?" He says glaring at me.

"Yo, Adam?" the person on the phone speaks again.

"I'll call you back, Rich," Adam says before hanging up. *Rich*. I'll have to remember that name. "The fuck is wrong with you, man?" He spits. When I don't say anything and just tilt my head, it sets him off.

He kicks open his car door and rushes out. My thumb found the switchblade button and with a satisfying click, the blade shot out. Adam stops in his tracks once he sees the blade.

"Can't start shit like a man? Gotta use a mask and a little pussy bitch knife. Pathetic," he says, shaking his head.

I chuckle and take a few steps forward, causing him to stumble backwards.

"Can't even show his pussy ass face either," his voice trembles. I kept walking towards him until he was pressed up against his car. Once I'm directly in front of him, I sigh and push my mask up, revealing my face.

"A-Alec?" he shudders.

"Adam," I say, tilting my head and grinning. I bring my knife up to his face, and the sharp edges catch the light. "So, here's the deal. I suggest you leave right now before I lose my temper with the way you just disrespected what belongs to me," I warn, and his eyes remain transfixed on the sharp blade in my hand.

"O-okay," he says, nodding.

"Say anything about what happened tonight, and I'll make sure you attend church every day.

From the ground" I hiss, taking a step back, letting him scramble into his car. Saying nothing, he peels out of the parking lot, leaving behind the sound of screeching tires.

Now, it's time to hunt.

CHAPTER SEVEN
HAYDEN

Finally, the carnival is dying down. I stand at the exit to the house of mirrors and tell whoever comes out, *"Happy Halloween, and have a good night."*

"Hayden, make sure you do a walk through after we close. Make sure no one tries pulling a fast one on us and hide somewhere in here," I hear Hank, the carnival's ringmaster says.

I smile and give him the thumbs up. "You got it!" I wait for everyone to leave before I close the exit door and lock it. Then I walk up to the entrance and pull out the directions Hank gave me for shutting down the attraction.

I. Shut the exit door first and lock it. In case there is someone in there, they can't get away.
II. Dim the lights, but don't turn them all the way off.

III. *To find your way through, use the UV light hanging up in the outside closet on the left of the entrance door. Shine it on the floor and you should see arrows show up. (Reason I said dim the lights) They lead the way through the maze.*

IV. *Please turn off all lights and music.*

V. *Close and lock the entrance door. You have to wiggle the key in the door a bit. Doors getting a little old.*

Okay, seems easy enough. I walk to the outside closet and open it. Spotting the flashlight, I grab it and then walk back to the entrance. I switch on the light and point it at the floor as I walk in. Arrows begin to glow. Well, would you look at that? That's pretty handy.

I walk through the house, following the arrows. I check everywhere. Every nook and cranny. I get to the exit door. Place is clear. I turn around and start heading back when the lights go out.

"What the fuck? Hello?" I say, stopping and looking around. I don't hear anything. I shine the flashlight onto the floor and follow the arrows out.

As I round a corner, the hairs on the back of my neck and arms stand up. I'm not alone.

"Hello? Kenna, if this is you playing games, I'm gonna kill you!" I shout, hoping my friend is just playing a trick on me. Then I see it. An orange glow is reflecting in one of the mirrors.

"Kenna?" I say, but it comes out as a whisper. The light gets brighter in the reflection. I keep my eye on it, waiting for whatever is making that light to show up. Why? I don't know. My body just won't move, no matter how hard I'm trying to.

I watch as the light comes closer and starts to light up the floor in front of me. An apparition comes around the corner, the dimness of the lights outlining their figure. Tall, broad shoulders, a man. He's walking slowly. The orange light is from a mask. The eyes are X's, and the mouth looks like it's supposed to be sowed shut. I stumble backwards as he keeps approaching me.

"Stop. W-were closed" I shudder. He continues to walk towards me. "Stop!" I shouted, continuing to step backwards. His pace picks up, so I turn and run. I try following the arrows and looking behind me at the same time. I round the corner to the exit door. Yes! I run and push on the door, but it doesn't budge.

"No," I scream, pounding on the door. I locked it, and it doesn't unlock from the inside. I keep pounding on the door with the flashlight and my fists, hoping someone will hear me.

Suddenly there's a hand around the back of my neck. I'm pulled backwards and spun around. Then slammed against the mirrored wall. The glowing orange mask is shining down on me. His hand is now wrapped around my throat, slowly tightening. I drop the flashlight and start hitting his arms and kicking at him. He laughs.

His laugh fades away and he leans in, and whispers in my ear, "Keep fighting me. You're only making me harder."

My body goes stiff. Because of what he just said, and his voice sounds familiar. "What do you want?" I whimper, holding onto his wrist, trying to pull him away. He chuckles.

“Use your imagination, baby. What do you think I want to do?”

“I don’t know! I don’t know what I did to you or who you even are!” I cry out.

“Oh Hayden,” he says, caressing my cheek. “You didn’t do anything wrong baby” he pauses and takes a deep breath and sighs. I feel his warm breath hitting my skin through the small holes in his mask. “And you’ll find out soon enough.”

“Please don’t” I beg. I thrash around again. I swung one of my hands out, smacking him. I feel the skin of his neck on one of the slaps. So, I slap him again and this time dig my nails into his skin and pull, ripping his skin open.

“Fuck!” he shouts. He loosens his grip as one of his hands flies to his neck. I take my chance and I kick at him, pushing him backwards. He stumbles, letting go of me. I ducked out of his reach and run for the flashlight. I grab it from the floor and point it at the floor and follow the arrows out.

CHAPTER EIGHT
ALEC

I pull my hand away and see it streaked with red. I smile and chuckle. I can hear her running. Zigzagging between the mirrors. Sometimes a catch sight of her and the look on her face makes my cock grow harder. I wipe my neck on my coat sleeve. I hiss from the burn of the fabric as it rubs against the tender skin.

I look in the direction Hayden ran and begin my pursuit. I see her reflection bouncing off mirrors and then disappearing. Her whimpers echo as they bounce off the glass.

I follow her out of the attraction and watch as she darts toward the corn maze. "You can't escape me!" I yell after her, my voice echoing through the empty carnival. As she disappears into the tall stalks, I shout after her once more, hoping she'll hear me. "Run baby run!"

I come to a stop outside the field, raise my mask, take a deep breath, let it out, and then lower it back down. I reach into my back pocket and pull out my switchblade and open it. A quick press of a button and the blade shoots out from the end of the handle.

Following the trail of flattened corn stalks, I pushed my way through the dense field. I hear the corn rustling in front of me, so I stop and look around. I see the corn moving slightly, then a crunch of a footstep follows closely behind.

"Gotcha," I say, charging in that direction. I burst through the stalks, grabbing Hayden from behind. She screams.

"No!" she cries and kicks as I wrap my arm around her waist and hold the knife to her neck with my other hand. I pull her up against my chest. Her body is shaking, and her nun costume is drenched in sweat. I groan at the feeling. I pull her in closer and grind my throbbing cock against her ass.

"Please stop," she cries, trying to twist around in my arms. My knife pierces her skin, causing a small trickle of blood to flow down the blade and fuck me. It's a beautiful sight.

I take the blade from her neck and drag it along the front of her costume. “You wore this for me, didn’t you?” I growl in her ear.

“I don’t even fucking know you!” she screams. She stomps on my feet and keeps trying to pull away.

“Oh, you will,” I say as I pull the knife away and force her to the ground. She tries to crawl away but fails as I pull her ankle yanking her back to me. I hold her down, straddling her hips. Her tiny fists pound against my chest, her small body writhing beneath me.

“Please, someone help me! Ah!” she begs and cries as she fights me. I go to reach into my coat when she smacks me hard across the face, causing my mask to fly off and my head to snap to the left. I feel her nails pierce my skin again.

“Oh, baby, you’re gonna pay for that.”

CHAPTER NINE
HAYDEN

I slap him, and I slap him hard. It sends his mask flying, and I feel my nails cut through his skin.

"Oh, baby, you're gonna pay for that," he growls. I still can't see his face. The corn stalks are blocking out the light from the lampposts. I watch his shadow lean up and watch as he reaches for something.

"Stop, please," I continue to beg. I hear what sounds like beads clacking together. What the fuck? He moves quickly, catching my wrists and bounding them together. I struggle against him, but it doesn't work. I can feel my body growing tired. The fight in me is slowly draining.

I feel the bulge of his cock grind against me as he secures my wrists. I squeeze my eyes shut and whimper.

"Why?" I choke out.

He laughs. Fucking laughs. "You know, I asked God that same exact thing. And you know what? He never answered, so here we are,"

I go to speak but stop when I hear the sound of his knife opening. My body trembles. He holds my bound wrists above my head. Then he moves his body off me and uses the tip of his knife to coax my knees apart. I let them fall open, and he settles between them.

"I fit perfectly between these soft thighs," he whispers, tracing the inside of my thigh with his blade, making his way towards my clothed center. I feel the cold metal graze on the outside of my panties.

My breath hitches as I gasp, "Stop."

He leans down to my ear and whispers. "By the end of this, you'll be desperate for me to keep going instead of stopping." He slips the knife under the fabric of my panties and pulls, cutting the fabric open. He forcefully tears away the remaining pieces, leaving a stinging sensation on my skin. He brings the knife back down and traces the slit of my pussy. With the very tip of the blade, he lightly touches my clit, causing me to shiver uncontrollably.

"Ow, fuck!" I cry out. He quickly replaces the tip of his knife with his thumb. He rubs me slowly, causing me to arch my hips towards him. Why is my body doing this to me?

"Is someone into knife play?" he whispers in my ear. His breath warms my neck as he speaks. Ignoring his questions, I twist my body and start kicking at the ground, trying to get away. His thumb abandons my clit, and my body starts to relax until I feel something cold and hard press against my entrance.

"W-what are you doing?" I scream. "Stop please!"

The cold, blunt object entered me slowly, causing unbearable pain, and I could feel tears streaming down my cheeks uncontrollably. It feels like I'm being slowly torn apart. He slowly pulls it out, then pushes it back in even further.

"We got to loosen this tight cunt up a little bit for me, baby," he groans as he pushes it in again. "You're dripping all over the handle of my blade."

My eyes widen. I go to scream, but it turns into an unwanted moan as he pulls the handle out and pushes it back in until it hits resistance. He stops as soon as he feels it. My heart pounding so hard I can feel it in my head.

"You saved that for me, didn't you?" he whispers.

"You fucking asshole!" I scream and throw myself around. My forehead connects with his nose.

"Ah fuck!" he shouts. He lets go of my wrists and sits up, pulling the knifes handle from me. My feet scrabble against the ground as I scoot away. As I flip over onto my knees and bound hands, I feel my arousal coating the inside of my thighs. I groan as I push myself up and book it out of there.

CHAPTER TEN

HAYDEN

I run and push stalks out of my way until I come out of the maze. I breathe heavily, looking around, trying to figure out where I am. I still haven't seen Adam anywhere. I can't believe that piece of shit ditched me!

Finally, I see a familiar church sign. I dart towards it, hoping someone's there. I run up the church's stairs and start pounding on the door.

"Father Greene!" I shout, continuing to bang on the door. "Father Greene!" I shout again. As I pound on the door with my bound hands, I look and see what's been holding my wrists together.

Rosary beads. I stop pounding on the door, pulling my wrists closer. The dimmed porch light of the church illuminated the black and shining beads. I follow the beads around my wrists until I find it. The crucifix.

"What the fuck- "

“He’s not here,” I hear a deep voice come from behind me. I spin around and slam my back against the door.

“Jesus,”

“Nope, just Alec,” Alec laughs. I sigh in relief at seeing a familiar face. He looks at me up and down and then zeroes in on my bounded wrists. He tilts his head in confusion. “Are you alright Hayden?” he asks, walking closer. Tears streamed down my face, and I couldn’t help but stare at the ground.

“No” I croak out. I hear him approach me, and then the sound of keys jingling.

“Come on, let’s get you inside,” he says as he reaches past me and unlocks the church’s door.

“Thank y-“ I start to say until I see the side of his cheek. It’s bleeding from scratches. Scratches I left. I go to scream but he muffles it with one of his hands and then opens and pushes me inside the door with the other. I pull away from him and run down the aisle lined with pews.

“Not this time,” I hear him say from right behind me. I feel him wrap his arms around my waist. He then picks me up and starts walking to the chancel. I wiggle and twist in his grip.

“Put me the fuck down!” my screams rattle off the church’s walls. He walks up the stairs of the chancel and walks over to the large cross. He walks closer to it and then I see it. There’s a long nail sticking out near the bottom. “No, no, stop!” I beg.

He throws me down to the floor, then grabs my wrists and drags me backwards towards the cross. “Alec please!”

CHAPTER ELEVEN

ALEC

I drag her towards the nail, where I plan to hang her. We get to the cross and I lift her up into a standing position. Holding her hands above her head, I wrap my arm around her waist, pulling her close to me lifting her. In one quick motion, I'm able to hang her wrists from the nail. I let her go and step back. She screams as the rosary beads dig and pinch at her skin as she dangles. Her toes barely touching the ground.

Perfect. I take another step back and take a deep breath and admire my work. Hayden's face is lit by the gentle glow of candlelight, the tears on her cheeks shimmering in the flickering light. She lost her veil and cap in the corn maze after our little tussle. Her short habit skirt is covered in dirt and corn silk from running through the stalks. Mud covers her heeled boots, and her stockings are torn.

I walk up to her and tilt her head up. Her eyes are red from crying and her bottom lip is quivering. Without thinking, I lean in, slamming my lips against hers. At first, she pulls back, but then leans in.

Finally, her lips are soft and taste salty from the tears that have fallen on them. I push my tongue through the seam of her mouth, deepening the kiss. I groan as our tongues tangle.

And then she does it. She bites my tongue. She pierces it with her teeth, then let's go. I pull away and look at her. Her lips are stained with my blood, and I can feel my cock hardening at the sight.

"You just love to make me bleed, don't you?" I say as I lean into her. She tries to kick out at me, but I grab her leg and wrap it around my hip. I feel the warmth of her bare pussy against the front of my pants, rubbing against my throbbing cock. I take the blade of my knife and bring it up to the collar of her dress. I push it under the hem and pull, cutting the material down the middle, revealing what she's wearing underneath.

My eyes lock on her beautiful tits, heaving up and down from her heavy panting. She's wearing a black laced bra. I wonder if her panties were matching? Hm, I might have to walk through the cornfield in the morning to find out.

Dying to see more of my blood on her, I grab her by the throat with my left hand and tilt her head away and dive in. Her skin is warm and salty as my bleeding tongue travels from her left breast to the side of her throat, leaving a trail of blood along the way. I suck and nibble at her neck. She whines, but it's followed by a moan. With my nose buried in the soft skin of her neck, I slid the knife under the fabric of her bra and cut through the material between the cups, exposing her naked chest.

"Fuck me," I mumbled as I lean back to get a look at them. They hang low, lower than they sat in her bra. Her nipples are a light shade of pink and are peaked. I lean down but keep my eyes lock on her face, as I wrap my lips around one of her nipples. Her mouth drops open, her eyes close, and she groans. I circle her nipple with my tongue then bit it lightly

"Ah fuck," she whispers. I can feel her swallow her moans under my hand that's wrapped around her throat still. I grin against her breast and pull back and look at my work.

"Perfect. But I know what'll make these feel and look even better," I whisper with a grin.

CHAPTER TWELVE

HAYDEN

"Perfect. But, I know what'll make these feel and look even better" he grins as he let's go of my throat, pulling away. I watch as he walks over to a table that's holding hundreds of candles and leaves me hanging. How have these beads lasted this long holding my weight?

"W-what?" I ask. He ignores me and continues to do whatever he's doing. Staring at his back, I feel my arousal slowly run down the inside of my thighs. I shouldn't be turned on by this, but I am. Fuck. And now that I know it's him, I'm even more turned on.

He takes off his coat and rolls up the sleeves of his black button-up shirt. I see the muscles on his back twitch as he moves. I feel my clit throb, causing my body to move involuntarily. The rosary beads jingle, and he turns his head towards me.

The side profile of his face shows how beautifully sculpted he is. He grins, then turns back to the table. I watch as he puts his knife in his back pocket, then turns towards me. He's holding a metal tray. What the fuck is that shit?

With one hand, he pulls the pulpit over next to us and sets the tray down on it.

Gloves and small packages of metal tools cover the tray. "What are you doing?" I ask as he grabs the gloves, stretching them over his hands, snapping each one on once they're covering his hand. He continues to ignore me. "Alec!" he still ignores me. I huff and kick out at the pulpit, but he snags my leg mid air. He grabs me by the cheeks and pulls me close to his face. He let's go of my leg and reaches for something out of my line of sight.

"Open," he growls, squeezing my cheeks hard. I clenched my jaw to keep it shut, but it just causes him to squeeze harder. I give in and open. I watch as he brings a white and gold cloth up to my face, then jamming it into my mouth, causing me to gag.

"Keep fucking around, and an alter cloth won't be the only thing gagging you," he whispers in my ear, then letting go, turning back to the pulpit. I close my eyes and lean my head back against the cross. I feel tears gathering, waiting to fall. I hear the sound of plastic rustling and metal clinking. I try to tone out the noises until something cold and wet touches one of my nipples.

My eyes open and I look down. Alec is cleaning the blood off the breast. He teases my nipple with the alcohol pad. My eyes roll to the back of my head and my body twitches as he keeps circling my nipple and rubbing my breast until it's clean of his blood.

He pulls away, and I whimper, the cloth muffling the sound. The cold air dances across my sensitive nipple, creating goosebumps to scatter across my body.

I feel his touch on me again. His gloved hands grab and give my breast a little squeeze, then something pinches me, and it hurts. I open my eyes and look down, watching his hand. I see a metal clamp pinched around my nipple, holding onto it. What the fuck?

Alec's other hand comes into view, and I see it. A needle.

"This might hurt a little," he grins, pushing the needle through. I scream into the cloth and flinch, my body jerking around. I squeeze my eyes shut and whimper. I feel him finish pushing the needle through and then pushing something else through. I'm assuming the jewelry he had planned. I feel the cold, wet sensation again. This time causing my nipple to burn.

I open my eyes and look down again. He pierced my nipple and put a hoop through it that has a cross dangling from it. The same cross that is on the rosary beads.

"Fuck, you're beautiful," he says as he stands back to admire his work. He pulls the gloves off and tosses them to the side. His fingers move slowly as he reaches up to unbutton his shirt. I watch as he slowly reveals his sculpted body. A trail of dark hair disappears into his pants. He shrugs the shirt off and tosses it to the side.

He walks up to me and grabs the cloth, slowly pulling it from my mouth. Once it's gone, I take an involuntary deep breath. His lips brush against mine, and he grabs both of my thighs and spreads them open, stepping between them. He keeps one hand wrapped around my thigh, keeping it hooked around his hip. His other hand travels down between us, and his rough fingers dip into my lips. I gasp and he grins. “See, I told you, you’d be begging for me,” he says.

I shake my head. “I’m not” I whisper. He takes his hand away and holds it up to my face. They’re soaked.

“You sure about that?” He slipped his finger in his mouth, cleaning my wetness off them. “So fucking sweet,” he groans. His hand dives back down between us, but he doesn’t touch me. Instead, he starts unbuckling his belt and undoing his pants. I struggle to resist the urge to look down, but my eyes betray me. I see him pull his pants down a bit, and suddenly his dick springs out, slapping against his abdomen. He’s long and thick. I see two silver balls at the top and bottom of the head of it.

Oh fuck.

I shake my head. Nope. Nope. Nope. “Alec, wait please” I beg. He ignores me and rubs his shaft up and down a few times.

“Father, forgive me,” he says with a heavy sigh, “for I am about to sin.”

CHAPTER THIRTEEN

HAYDEN

My eyes grow wide. Alec lines himself up with my entrance and slowly pushes in.

"Ah!" I cry out in pain. It's too much. It's all too much. The pressure and the burning. "Stop it's too much!"

Surprisingly, he stops and looks at me. He cups my cheeks and leans in, claiming my lips.

Suddenly, he stops and pulls out, leaving only the head of his cock inside me. I feel his hand move from my cheek to my throat, squeezing tightly.

Time feels like it stops as we scan each other's faces. Then he slams into me, breaking me open. I open my mouth and try to scream, but the grip Alec has around my throat silences me.

"Oh, fuck," he groans, continuing to pound in and out of me. All I feel is pain. My stomach's cramping and the burning gets worse.

He let's up on the hold he has on my throat, and I take a deep breath. "That's it, baby. Relax, breathe through it. It'll feel good soon," he moans into my ear.

My body is too tired to fight, so I give in. All the way in. My legs relax and open wider for him, making him pound deeper into me. He lets go of my throat and brings his hand down between us. He alternates between pinching my clit and rubbing it in gentle circles, sending waves of pleasure through my body.

"Oh, God" I moan. The pain turns into pleasure. The cramps in my stomach fade away.

"That's right, baby. I'm your fucking God now. I want all your confessions, all your sins. I want every. Single. Fucking part of you. All of it. And if I gotta commit one of the biggest sins and knock you up to keep you. Then so be it." Alec moans as he fucks me.

I feel myself start clenching around him. He suddenly stops and pulls out, but I'm filled back up with something hard and cold... his knife. I pick my head back up and look at him. He's looking down to where we were just connected. I look as well. His dick and lower abs are covered in my innocence, and now his knife handle is, too. He pushes a button on the knife handle, retracting the blade. Then he lines his cock up with my entrance again, but this time under the handle... that's still inside me.

"Alec, don't you fucking dare-" I'm cut short as I watch Alec push himself in. I scream. He pushes himself in until both him and the knife are deep inside.

"Holy fuck" Alec groans. I'm shaking uncontrollably. I look up at him and whimper.

"It's too much, please," I beg. What am I begging for? No fucking clue.

Alec grins and holds the end of the knife that's barely sticking out of me. Then he fucks me again. The handle and his dick, stretching me wide open. He keeps the knife still while he thrusts into me.

His balls slap against my ass as he takes me roughly.

"It's time for you to come on my knife and cock, baby," he whispers to me. With a firm grip on my thigh, he pulls me towards him and changes the angle, sending waves of pleasure through my body. I throw my head back as I feel something so weird but so good flowing through my body. My pussy starts clenching around Alec and the knife, making every move feel tighter.

"Ah! Fuck Alec!" I scream as I feel pressure, then a sudden burst of pleasure hits me and I come with a scream. I throw my head back as I slowly come down off my high, my pussy still spasming around him.

"Fuck, you're soaking me right now," Alec growls. His thrusts get harder and erratic, and then he slams in hard and holds himself there.

He comes with a groan and pulls me into him and rests his forehead against mine. I feel his cock twitching, emptying inside me. We stay molded together, panting, staring into each other's eyes.

"I better see you Sunday morning sitting that pretty little tight ass in that front pew," he whispers.

EPILOGUE

ALEC

It's Sunday morning and I'm standing behind my father, who is standing at the pulpit, waiting for everyone to come in and take their seats. I look at the front pew and smile. Hayden gives me a little smile, then looks away. I clear my throat and open my bible waiting for my father to begin his prayers. He looks back at me and nods, letting me know he's about to begin. I look at Hayden one more time and wonder, will she have any confessions for me later?

THE END

FOR NOW...

COMING SOON

ACKNOWLEDGEMENTS

I want to start off by saying thank you to my husband Tator for always supporting me and helping me with "things" ;)

And I also want to say THANK YOUUUU TO MY GIRL ANGEL. THANK YOU. Thank you for always listening to me brain storm about my book ideas and then giving your honest opinion on things and helping me with ideas. I'm so fucking happy that we've gotten so close. I LOVE YOU.

And, I want to say thank you to you, the reader. Thank you for taking the time to read my books!

BOOKS BY THIS AUTHOR

CAUGHT IN THE CROSSFIRE

DELILAH

I was at the wrong place at the wrong time, and unfortunately, when that happens, sometimes it comes with baggage. And man, oh man, did mine come with “baggage”. Tall, dark, and handsome baggage. Issac Raven and his motorcycle club saved me when I was in the wrong place, but little did I know that day would change everything in my life. Especially when the person you become attracted to becomes your frenemy...

ISSAC

She wasn't supposed to be there. She wasn't supposed to be the only thing I thought about all the time. I was only supposed to help her heal and move on... but sometimes things just don't work that way. Especially with the life I live. And now Delilah has become a pawn in a game my clubs rivals are playing, but little do they know I will protect her at any cost. Even if it comes to my family...

This book ends on a cliff hanger!

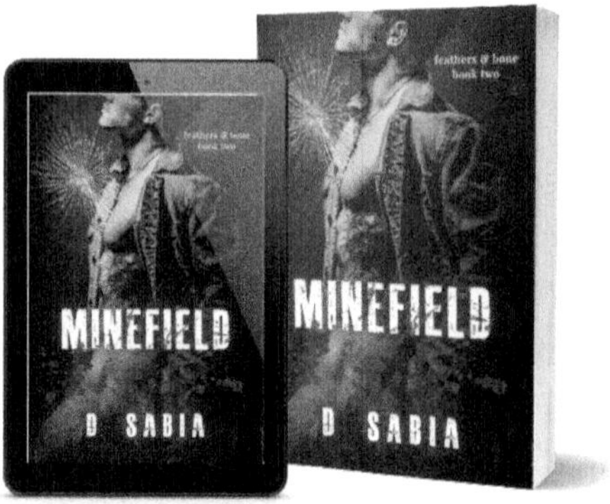

MINEFIELD

ISSAC

We fought, and we survived. But in the end I failed to protect her. I promised her I'd never let anything happen to her, and I broke it. And because of this, I might lose the love of my life. But you know what they always say;

"If you love them, let them go....

But I'm never letting go.

Never again.

TRIGGER WARNINGS

Each book includes graphic references to topics such as sexual abuse, self-harm, violence, murder, and graphic sexual scenes. These books are recommended for audiences 18 and up.

Printed in Great Britain
by Amazon

50600504R00040